You're All My Favourites

Sam McBratney

Ani ram

WALKER BO
AND SUBSIDIARIES
LONDON · BOSTON · SYDNEY ·

Once upon a time

there was a mother bear,

a father bear

and three baby bears.

A first baby bear. A second baby bear.

And a third baby bear.

Whoever tucked them in at night

always said the same thing to them:

"You are the most wonderful baby bears

in the whole wide world!"

One night, after their Mummy Bear

had tucked them in, and after she had said

"You are the most wonderful baby bears

in the whole wide world",

the baby bears began to wonder.

"But how do you know?" they asked

their Mummy Bear. "How do you know

we are the most wonderful baby bears

in the whole wide world?"

"Because your daddy told me,"

said their Mummy Bear.

"When your daddy saw you on the night

that you were born, he said —

and I remember it very well — he said,

'Those are the nicest baby bears

I have ever seen.

They are the nicest baby bears

anyone has ever seen!'"

That was a good answer.

The three baby bears snuggled

down as content as could be.

But one day, the first baby bear
began to think. He wondered if the
other two bears were better than he was.
They had patches, after all,
and he did not. Maybe his mummy
really really liked patches.

And the second baby bear began to wonder.

Maybe daddy loves the other two

more than me, she thought.

They were boy bears, after all,

and she was not.

And the third baby bear

began to worry.

I'm only the littlest, he thought.

Everybody's bigger than me!

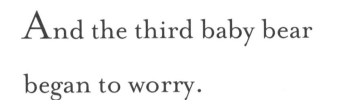

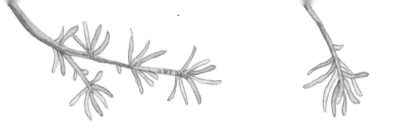

So that night the three baby bears asked their Daddy Bear,

"But which one of us do you like most?

Who is your favourite?

We can't all be the best."

"Yes you can," said their Daddy Bear. "I know you can because I heard your mummy say so. When she saw you" — and Daddy Bear picked up the first baby bear to give him a cuddle — "she said, 'That is the most perfect first little bear that anyone has ever seen.'"

"Even with no patches?"

"Patches don't matter at all," replied his daddy, as he tucked him in.

"And when your mummy saw you" – Daddy Bear
picked up the second baby bear – "she said,

'That is the most perfect
second little bear that
anyone has ever seen.'"

"Even if I'm not a boy?"

"Girl or boy, it makes
no difference," said
her daddy, and he
hugged her tight.

"And when your mummy saw you" — Daddy Bear

lifted the last baby bear into his arms —

"she said, 'That is the most perfect third

little bear that anyone has ever seen.'"

"Even if I'm the littlest?"

"Biggly or littley,

we love you just the same.

So there. Three favourites.

You're all my favourites!"

And the best baby bears in the whole wide world

went to sleep as happily as could be, because

that was a good answer too.

For all *my* favourites:
Sam and Daniel and Jack
and Adam and Ella   ~ *S. McB.*

For Joe, Danny and Kitty   ~ *A. J.*

First published 2004 by Walker Books Ltd
87 Vauxhall Walk, London SE11 5HJ

This edition including DVD published 2007

4 6 8 10 9 7 5

Text © 2004 Sam McBratney
Illustrations © 2004 Anita Jeram

The right of Sam McBratney and Anita Jeram to be identified
as author and illustrator respectively of this work has been asserted by them
in accordance with the Copyright, Designs and Patents Act 1988

This book has been typeset in Mrs Eaves

Printed in China

British Library Cataloguing in Publication Data:
a catalogue record for this book is available from the British Library

ISBN 978-1-4063-0740-5

www.walkerbooks.co.uk

JAN BRETT
The Hat

MACDONALD YOUNG BOOKS

For Sam and Joshua Carty

Copyright © Jan Brett 1997

First published in Great Britain in 1998 by
Macdonald Young Books
an imprint of Wayland Publishers Ltd
61 Western Road
Hove
East Sussex
BN3 1JD

Find Macdonald Young Books on the internet at http://www.myb.co.uk

First published by G P Putnam's Sons
a division of The Putnam & Grosset Group
200 Madison Avenue
New York, NY 10016

Printed and bound in Portugal by Edições ASA
British Library Cataloguing in Publication Data available.

ISBN: 0 7500 2604 9

Winter was on the way. Lisa took her woollen
clothes out of the chest and carried them outside.

She was hanging them up in the fresh air, when
a strong wind blew one of her socks off the line.

Curious Hedgie found it and poked his nose in. When he pulled it out, the sock was stuck on his prickles. "How embarrassing," Hedgie thought.

The mother hen came by with her chicks.
"Cackle, cackle," she clucked and laughed.
"What's that on your head, Hedgie?"

"Why it's my new hat," he told her. "Isn't it beautiful?"
The mother hen cocked her head as if she had an idea.
And off she ran.

Hedgie saw the noisy gander looking down at him.
"Honk, honk! Ho, ho, ho!" the gander laughed.
"Look at that! The hedgehog has flipped his gizzard."
"Laugh today, Gander. But tomorrow when it rains,
my hat will keep me dry."
The gander thought for a moment. And off he ran.

The barn cat was watching from a tree as Hedgie tugged at the sock.

"Miaow," he called down. "What a silly-looking hedgehog you are, with that thing on your head."

"But my ears will be warm in a snowstorm."

"Hmmmmm," purred the cat. And off he ran.

The farm dog and her puppies found Hedgie in a patch of brambles.

"Hedgie, is that a hat you're wearing? How funny you look," she barked, and her puppies yelped and giggled.

"But I'll be cosy and dry when it snows,"
Hedgie said.
The farm dog's ears perked up. And off she ran.

"Oink, oink!" the piglets squealed.
"What are you up to, Hedgie?" the mummy pig asked.

"Making sure my hat doesn't fall off
if an icy wind blows up."

"I see," said the mummy pig. And off she ran.

"Hedgie, what is that ridiculous thing on your head?" the pony snorted at Hedgie. That was the last straw.

"It's my hat, of course. Don't you know that everyone should wear a hat in winter when it's cold and snowy!" Hedgie shouted.

The pony looked startled. Hedgie was usually so friendly. And off he ran.

Hedgie just wanted to be alone. He was tired of
everyone laughing at him, and with this thing on
his head, couldn't even fit in his den.

He didn't see Lisa running after him, with the other sock in her hand.

"Come back, you silly hedgehog," she called.

"Oh no," Hedgie thought.
"Even the girl is laughing at me!"

Lisa caught up and pulled her sock off Hedgie's head.
"You ridiculous little hedgehog," she laughed.
"Don't you know that animals don't wear clothes!"

Hedgie headed for his den, and Lisa started back towards the clothes-line. That's when she saw all of her missing woollens.

The animals had taken
them and each one was thinking,
"Now *I* am wearing a magnificent hat!"

Lisa was still chasing them when Hedgie reached his den.

"How ridiculous they look! Don't they know that animals should never wear clothes!"